Ben's Rocket

by Anne Cassidy

Illustrated by Steve Cox

W

FRANKLIN WATTS

First published in 2015 by
Franklin Watts
338 Euston Road
London
NW1 3BH

Franklin Watts Australia
Level 17/207 Kent Street
Sydney
NSW 2000

A CIP catalogue record for this book is available
from the British Library.

ISBN 978 1 4451 3790 2 (hbk)
ISBN 978 1 4451 3793 3 (pbk)
ISBN 978 1 4451 3792 6 (library ebook)
ISBN 978 1 4451 3791 9 (ebook)

Series Editor: Jackie Hamley
Series Advisor: Catherine Glavina
Series Designer: Peter Scoulding

Printed in China

Franklin Watts is a division of
Hachette Children's Books,
an Hachette UK company.
www.hachette.co.uk

For Ben –
lots of love, A.C.

Ben wanted to go into space.

He had a space suit.

He built a rocket.

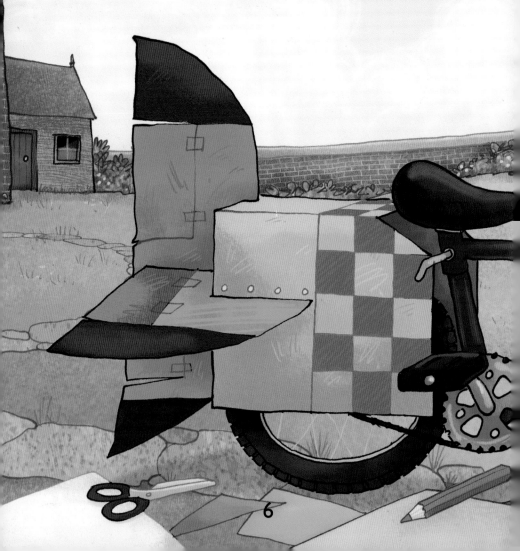

He tried to take off.

But he landed in
the sandpit.

11

Ben got some balloons.

The balloons didn't take him high enough.

"I'll show you space,"
his dad said.

Ben looked through the telescope.

"Wow!" he said.
"Look at those stars!"

Ben was happy.

Maybe one day he would go into space!

Puzzle Time!

Put these pictures in the right order and tell the story!